4/11

● Other

Shorewood – Troy Library
650 Deerwood Drive
Shorewood, IL 60404
815-725-1715

D1503173

KAZAAK!

Sean Cassidy

SHOREWOOD-TROY LIBRARY
650 DEERWOOD DRIVE
SHOREWOOD, IL 60404

Fitzhenry & Whiteside

Text and illustrations copyright © 2010 by Sean Cassidy

Published in Canada by Fitzhenry & Whiteside,
195 Allstate Parkway, Markham, Ontario L3R 4T8
Published in the United States by Fitzhenry & Whiteside,
311 Washington Street, Brighton, Massachusetts 02135

All rights reserved. No part of this book may be reproduced in any manner without the
express written consent of the publisher, except in the case of brief excerpts in critical
reviews and articles. All inquiries should be addressed to Fitzhenry & Whiteside Limited,
195 Allstate Parkway, Markham, Ontario L3R 4T8.

www.fitzhenry.ca   godwit@fitzhenry.ca

10 9 8 7 6 5 4 3 2 1

Library and Archives Canada Cataloguing in Publication
Cassidy, Sean, 1947-
    Kazaak! / Sean Cassidy.
ISBN 978-1-55455-117-0
    1. Porcupines—Juvenile fiction. I. Title.
PS8555.A78122K39 2010   jC813'.6   C2010-904387-1

U.S. Publisher Cataloging-in-Publication Data (Library of Congress Standards)
Cassidy, Sean.
    Kazaak! / Sean Cassidy.
[32] p. : col. ill. ; cm.
Summary: Spike is just learning about his new quills from his friend Rupert, but when Rupert
gets in trouble with Bear, Spike must use his imagination and his own quills to save him.
ISBN-13: 978-1-55455-117-0
1. Porcupines – Juvenile fiction. 2. Bears – Juvenile fiction. I. Title.
[E] dc22 PZ7.C37753Ka   2010

Fitzhenry & Whiteside acknowledges with thanks the Canada Council for the Arts, and
the Ontario Arts Council for their support of our publishing program. We acknowledge
the financial support of the Government of Canada through the Book Publishing Industry
Development Program (BPIDP) for our publishing activities.

Canada Council   Conseil des Arts
for the Arts   du Canada

ONTARIO ARTS COUNCIL
CONSEIL DES ARTS DE L'ONTARIO

Design by Kong Njo
Printed in Hong Kong, China

Teachers and parents: For FREE downloads and more amazing information about
porcupines, visit www.fitzhenry.ca.

To Maureen and Rol,
Ruth and Mike,
Linda and Jon,
with love

Spike is cleaning his quills for the very first time. He runs his tongue along a quill—right to the pointy end.

"YOW!" he shrieks.

"Quills are sharp!"

"Quills are the best," says Rupert.
"And they keep us porcupines safe."

"Teeth and claws can keep us safe,"
says Spike.

"Lots of animals have teeth and claws,
but quills can do much more. Watch."

Rupert scoots into a patch of weeds.
"You've almost disappeared!"
exclaims Spike.

He raises his nose and sniffs. "Bear is in the woods.
I will hide with you."

"Bear is afraid of quills," says Rupert. "And the woods
are full of juicy treats. Come on!"

"Wild grapes are juicy," says Spike.

"Watch me spear them with my quills," says Rupert.

He swings his tail in a mighty arc.

K A

ZAAK!

"See? The juice trickles down the quills
and into your mouth."
"Tastes yummy," says Spike.

Spike sniffs the air again. "Will we hear Bear before he comes too close?"

"Bear will hear us first. Listen." Rupert shakes his quills. *CHIK-chik, CHIK-chik, CHIK-chik.*

Spike laughs, "We will frighten Bear away."

CHIK-chik

CHIK-chik

CHIK-chik

The scent of Bear still tingles in Spike's nose.

"What if Bear still finds us? What if Bear *isn't* frightened away?"

"Then I will KAZAAK that Bear. Watch!"

Rupert tugs out a root.

"That smells like a carrot," says Spike.

"I'll KAZAAK it." Rupert swings his tail in a mighty arc.

KAZAAK!

KAZAAK!

He smashes into the root.
He smashes it again.

"Quills are the best!" he cheers.

KAZAAK!

"Quills can even do magic,"
says Rupert. "Watch!"

Rupert trots up to an old tree.
He turns around and jumps.

His quills sink deep into the bark.

"WOW!" cheers Spike. "But how
do you get yourself unstuck?"

KAZAAK!

Rupert wiggles against the tree.
Bit by bit, he comes unstuck.
"You've lost so many quills!"
says Spike. "Do you have any left?"
"I can always grow more,"
says Rupert.

"Ah! LUNCH!" growls Bear.

"Run away! Run away!" screams Spike.

"Wait, Spike. We can use our QUILLS!"

Rupert crouches low. He raises his tail and arches his back. He shakes from side to side.

Spike crouches low. He raises his tail and arches his back. He shakes from side to side.

"Go away," Rupert warns, "or I will KAZAAK you."
Rupert swings his tail in a mighty arc.

KAZAAK!

But Bear just laughs, "That tickles. KAZAAK me again!"

Spike peeks over Rupert's shoulder. "Oh dear," he says. Bear howls with glee. "KAZAAK me one more time," he begs, "before I gobble you for lunch."

"You can't eat me! You will hurt yourself. I have too many pointy quills!" says Rupert.

Bear chuckles, "Your little friend has pointy quills. You have none."

"Wait!" hollers Spike. "Rupert is VERY prickly. But HIS quills are still on the inside, ready to slide out."

Bear studies Rupert.
"Can this be true?"
he wonders. "You look
soft enough to me."

"Why, of course!" says Spike. "When you shed your fur in springtime, what's inside you, waiting to grow out?"

"More fur," says Bear, poking Rupert.

"Yes! Bears have fur," says Spike. "But Rupert is a porcupine.
What do you think is inside HIM waiting to grow out?"
"More QUILLS!" says Bear. "YUUCCKK!"

Bear grumbles, "But now I still have to find my lunch."

Spike giggles, "I'll KAZAAK these grapes for you."

Spike and Rupert climb into the top boughs of a tree.

Rupert says, "Thanks for saving me from that silly Bear."

"I can keep you safe until your new quills grow," says Spike.

"Because quills are the best!"

KA

WOULD YOU LIKE TO BE A PORCUPINE?

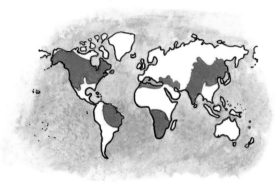

Porcupines live in North America, South America, Africa, Europe and Asia.

Porcupines are nocturnal. During the day, they sleep in safe places like hollow logs, small caves, or high up in trees. At night, they wake up and feed.

Porcupines Love Vegetables

In summer, they enjoy seeds, stems, and leaves or flowers of many plants, including water plants.

In winter, there are no leaves or flowers. Porcupines cannot dig for roots in the frozen ground. Ice covers the ponds and streams.

In winter, porcupines eat conifer needles and the inner bark of many trees, especially pine trees. They chew through the tough outer bark to get to the soft inner bark. Their teeth leave small marks on the wood where they have chewed.

YOU CAN DRAW A PORCUPINE

Draw a circle.

Add a curve for the snout.

Add a large circle.

Add legs with triangles for feet.

Draw a tail.

Quills

A porcupine has more than thirty thousand quills to keep it safe from other animals. Each quill has little barbs along its side. The barbs expand in body heat and make the quill difficult to pull out.

The quills are attached loosely to the skin. Porcupines do not throw their quills. If an animal gets too close, the porcupine flips its tail up and pushes the loose quills into the animal threatening it.

How long does it take to draw 30,000 quills?

If you drew two quills every second, it would take more than four hours to draw thirty thousand quills.

Porcupine Tracks

When a porcupine walks, its hind foot usually lands right in front of the spot that its front foot has just left. Its heavy tail often scratches lines in the earth.

Erase some lines.
Add nose, eye and mouth.

Draw a few guide quills.

Add lots of quills.

SHOREWOOD-TROY LIBRARY